Wolfman Sam

Also by Elizabeth Levy

Wolfman Sam

by Elizabeth Levy

illustrated by Bill Basso

HarperTrophy
A Division of HarperCollinsPublishers

Wolfman Sam
Text copyright © 1996 by Elizabeth Levy
Illustrations copyright © 1996 by HarperCollins Publishers
Printed in the United States of America. For information
address HarperCollins Children's Books, a division of
HarperCollins Publishers, 10 East 53rd Street, New York, NY 10022.

Library of Congress Cataloging-in-Publication Data
Levy, Elizabeth.
  Wolfman Sam / by Elizabeth Levy ; illustrated by Bill Basso.
    p.   cm.
  Summary: When Sam becomes "Wolfman Sam" as a disc jockey for the
school radio station, his brother Robert tricks him into thinking he really may
be a werewolf.
  ISBN 0-06-024817-3 (lib. bdg.). — ISBN 0-06-442048-5 (pbk.)
  [1. Disc jockeys—Fiction.   2. Werewolves—Fiction.]   I. Basso, Bill, ill.
II. Title.
PZ7.L5827Wo   1996   96-2542
[Fic]—dc20   CIP
                                                                              AC

1   2   3   4   5   6   7   8   9   10
❖
First Edition

To the memory of
the one and only Wolfman,
Robert Weston Smith,
the original Wolfman Jack.
To all the early rock-and-roll disc jockeys
who taught a girl from Buffalo, New York,
that there was something joyous
to howl about in the 1950's.
—E.L.

Contents

1

Hairy Armpits

"I can be heard but not seen. I won't speak unless I'm spoken to. Who am I?"

"ECHO ELMER! ECHO ELMER!" shouted Sam Bamford to the voice booming over his radio. His brother, Robert, stood in the doorway of Sam's room. Robert put his hands over his ears. Sam's mother came roaring into Sam's room. She turned down the radio.

"You'll wake the dead!" she said.

1

"You'll wake Mabel," giggled Robert. Recently, Robert and Sam's cousin Mabel and her family had moved to New York City from San Francisco. They had found an apartment just a block away. Ever since their arrival, they'd been complaining about the noise in New York City.

Sam loved noise—at least he loved the noise that came from the morning radio. It was the only way Sam could get up in the morning. Lately Sam had been sleeping really soundly.

"Mom! Please let me listen!" wailed Sam.

"You sound like one of your whiny songs," said Robert, who thought the music Sam listened to was boring. Echo Elmer loved early rock and rhythm and blues.

"Sam," said Mrs. Bamford, shutting off the radio, "I'm glad you've found something that helps you get up in the morning. But there's a limit. Besides, it's time to get ready. You don't want to be late."

Sam got up and went to take a shower. After a while Robert banged on the door. He really needed the bathroom. Sam couldn't hear him. Robert tried the knob. Sam had forgotten to lock the door. Robert walked in. It was like entering a spooky underwater cave. The steam from the hot water made it hard to see.

Hot water beat down on Sam. Sam sang as he washed under his arms. Suddenly he yelled, "Ouch!" Then he looked under his arm.

Sam jumped out of the shower, practically stepping on Robert. "What are you doing here?" Sam demanded.

"You were hogging the bathroom," said Robert indignantly.

"Out of my way, little boy," said Sam. "I've got to check something out." Sam wiped the steam away from the mirror. He looked under his arm.

"Are you trying to imitate a baboon?" asked Robert.

"No. Look at this. Today I am a man." Sam stuck his armpit in Robert's face.

Robert ran out of the bathroom. "Ma! Sam's making me sniff his pits!" he shouted.

Sam followed his brother into the kitchen with a towel around his waist.

"What's going on?" asked Mrs. Bamford.

Sam suddenly looked shy. He whispered something to his mother.

"Really?" asked Sam's mother. She looked under Sam's armpit.

"My whole family's weird!" muttered Robert, putting his head in his hands.

Mrs. Bamford smiled. "Sam just got his first underarm hair," she said.

Sam examined his armpit. "We've been studying this stuff in Ms. Perretti's class," he said.

"You're studying how to grow hair under your arm?" asked Robert. "I don't ever want to be in fifth grade."

"It's a sign of puberty," said Sam proudly. "You won't have to worry about this stuff until much later."

Mrs. Bamford was looking at Sam with a half-proud, half-sad expression on her face. "I guess my little boy is growing up. Early puberty runs in our family. My father told me that he had to shave when he was just a young teenager—and so did his grandfather."

"Mom, will you quit looking at Sam with that goofy expression?" complained Robert. "I don't think one little hair is such a big deal."

Mrs. Bamford grinned. "It'll happen to you soon enough," she said.

"I hope not," muttered Robert.

"I'm starving," said Sam. "Mom, can I have bacon and eggs, please?"

Mrs. Bamford chuckled. "Well, you are a growing boy," she said. "What kind of eggs do you want?"

"Green eggs and ham, Sam I am," said Robert.

"Scrambled. That joke is so juvenile," Sam said to Robert. "Mom, can you make my eggs runny? I don't like them cooked too long."

"Yuck!" said Robert, when Sam's eggs were done. "Your eggs look raw."

"It's delicious. Thanks, Mom," said Sam. "Come on, Robert. We'll be late."

Robert gave his brother a dirty look. After all, if they were going to be late, it was Sam's fault—for making such a fuss about his armpit and for wanting yucky-looking eggs. Yet Sam was blaming him. Typical Sam.

2

The First Bite

Mabel was waiting for them in the lobby of her building. She was dressed all in green. She had on green leggings, a green sweatshirt, and a green baseball cap.

"You look like broccoli," said Robert.

Mabel acted like she hadn't heard him.

"Hey, Green Vegetable, how's it going?" asked Sam. He poked Mabel in the arm.

Mabel turned around. "Were you talking to

me?" she asked. She took out the earplugs she had in her ears.

"Why are you wearing earplugs to school?" Sam asked her.

"The noise! The noise! It's killing me."

Sam put a letter in the mailbox.

"Who's the letter to?" asked Mabel, who was often nosy.

"We had to write a formal letter to someone we didn't know for English class," answered Sam. "Most kids picked authors. I picked Echo Elmer. I asked him if he'd be the disc jockey at the Monster Mash. Did you know Echo Elmer graduated from our school?"

"What's the Monster Mash?" asked Mabel.

"It's the Halloween dance for fourth and fifth graders only," said Sam. "You and Robert can't come."

"That's not fair," said Mabel.

"Who wants to go to the Monster Mash anyway?" said Robert. "I hear boys dance with girls—yuck!"

"Little Bro, you've got a lot to learn," said Sam.

Robert hated it when Sam called him Little Bro. "Sam, you won't need a costume for

Halloween," said Robert. "At the rate you're growing hair, you can be a werewolf."

"Yeah? Well, the first person I'd bite would be you," said Sam.

Mabel had a disgusted look on her face. She wrinkled her nose. "What's that smell?" she asked. "It smells like throw-up. New Yorkers just throw up all over the street."

Sam and Robert looked at each other. They had been born in New York, and they hated it when people, especially Mabel, put their city down.

Sam kicked a greenish nut that had fallen on the sidewalk. "It's just a ginkgo nut," he said. "Ginkgo trees grow really well in New York City. We learned that in environmental science. They're originally from China, and some people think ginkgo nuts are a great delicacy."

"Well, I think they stink," said Mabel.

"Hey Mabel, do you know why the squirrels spend so much time in trees?" asked Robert.

"No," said Mabel.

"To get away from nuts like you on the ground," said Robert. He giggled. Sam gave him a low five.

When they got closer to school, Sam ran into some of his classmates.

"See you later, Little Bro," said Sam. "Hey, Armando. Wait up! I've got something to tell you," shouted Sam.

"Oh, no," groaned Robert. "You're not going to tell people about your armpit. This is so embarrassing."

Sam ignored Robert. He cupped his hand over his mouth and whispered something to Armando. Armando started to laugh.

"What's the secret?" demanded Mabel. "It's not polite to whisper in front of someone."

"Believe me, you don't want to know," said Robert.

Robert watched as Armando and Sam said hello to a girl in their class. Sam chewed his lip. Robert thought he looked like a cow. The girl, Rebecca, just chattered way as if she didn't mind the fact that Sam didn't seem to have anything to say.

"I wish *we* could go to the Monster Mash for Halloween," said Mabel.

"It's got girls in it," said Robert.

"I'm a girl," Mabel pointed out.

"You're a relative. It's different," said Robert.

3

That's a Put-Down

Sam didn't hear from Echo Elmer for two weeks. He pretended that he didn't mind. He told himself that Echo Elmer was busy. Sam had other things to worry about. The Monster Mash was getting close. He wanted to ask Rebecca, but first he had to get up the nerve. Soon it might be too late.

Then one day the principal announced over the PA system that there would be an assembly.

The entire school marched into the auditorium. Mabel and Robert were in the same class, so they sat together. They could see Sam's class sitting way on the other side of the room. Standing next to the principal was a short man with big red-framed glasses. He was wearing a beige, neatly pressed suit.

The principal announced that their guest of honor would lead them in the pledge of allegiance. "I pledge allegiance . . ." boomed out a voice. There was no mistaking that voice.

Sam jumped up to get a better look. "That's Echo Elmer!" he shouted. Then he sat down quickly.

But Sam had to admit that Echo Elmer wasn't what he expected. He had pictured a wild guy with long hair in a ponytail. But Sam thought it was great that Echo Elmer wore glasses. After all, Sam wore glasses too.

The principal said he had an exciting announcement. "Echo Elmer *asked* to come to our school. He called and said he wanted to be the disc jockey for the Monster Mash, so this year's dance should be especially great. But I also asked Echo Elmer to come to school for Career Week and tell us what it's like to have a career in radio. So please give a nice hand to Mr. Elmer!" The principal turned the microphone over to Echo Elmer.

"It's good to be back at P.S. 11. Thank you to Sam Bamford for writing and inviting me."

Sam felt himself turn beet red, but Rebecca patted him on the back. "Way to go, Sam," she whispered.

"The best way to learn about a radio station is to run one. So I'm going to help you set up a morning radio program right through your PA system," said Echo Elmer. "We'll hold auditions for disc jockey, and I hope many of you will try out. Disc jockeys are part of music's history. Why, the very words 'rock and roll' came from a disc jockey, Alan Freed. He broadcast out of WJW in Cleveland, Ohio. That's why the Rock and Roll Hall of Fame is in Cleveland. One of the best-known disc jockeys was Wolfman Jack. He played only the finest blues—and he spent the night howling at the moon between and during records. He'd play Howlin' Wolf. Why, he was just the best!"

"There are an awful lot of wolves in this music, aren't there?" said Armando. He let out

a howl. Everybody laughed except Sam and his teachers. Sam thought Echo Elmer was great.

Sam couldn't wait to get home and start practicing for the auditions. He worked alone in his room all afternoon.

Just before dinner Sam went to the refrigerator. "I'm starved," he said. He frowned as he browsed through the refrigerator.

"Dinner will be ready soon. We're having pasta with fresh mushrooms. Have some fruit," said Mrs. Bamford.

Sam shook his head. "Naw—I'm really hungry. How come we never have anything you can sink your teeth into—like a steak?"

"You know we don't eat much red meat," said Mrs. Bamford.

"But that's what I feel like," said Sam. He grabbed a banana. "Oh well, maybe this will hold me till dinner. Now don't anybody come into my room. I'm working out my routine."

"What routine?" asked Mrs. Bamford.

"I'm going to try out for the morning disc jockey in our school. Echo Elmer is having auditions."

"You're going to bomb," said Robert.

Sam growled at his brother and bared his teeth.

"Ma! Sam's growling at me."

"Sam," said Mrs. Bamford, "don't growl at your brother."

"Robert put me down," complained Sam. "I thought one of the rules of the house was no put-downs," said Sam.

"It is," said Mrs. Bamford.

"I was just telling you the truth," said Robert. "You're awful when you have to perform. Not like me. Remember how good I was as Abraham Lincoln in my class play? With that great fake beard, my teacher said I was the spitting image of old Abe—didn't he, Mom?"

"Abe Lincoln was famous for being ugly," said Sam.

"That was a put-down too," said Robert. But he said it to Sam's back. Sam was already on his way to his room to practice.

4

Have Mercy!

A lot of kids lined up for the auditions for disc jockey. Mabel was dressed in a bright-pink outfit. "I wanted to stand out," she explained to Sam and Robert.

"It's radio, Mabel," said Sam disgustedly. He sounded nervous.

Echo Elmer came out to talk to the kids who had come for the auditions. "The most important thing is to sound relaxed on the radio. If you sound nervous, you'll make your audience nervous. Even if you are jittery, a good radio person learns to fake it. Now, I'm asking you all to introduce a piece of music that you like. Okay, let's have the first one on our sign-up sheet. Armando Warrick."

"That's me!" said Armando—except that it came out more like a croak.

Armando touched the microphone. It squeaked.

"Just relax," instructed Echo Elmer. "When I point my finger at you, it means it's time for you to introduce your song."

When Armando introduced his song, his voice cracked.

"It's okay," said Echo Elmer. "Tell us something about your group."

"They're the greatest!" said Armando.

Echo Elmer spread his arms wide. "And . . . what else?"

"And what?" asked Armando. "They're just the greatest."

"Next!" shouted Echo Elmer.

Armando came out looking dejected. "I don't

think he liked me. I thought it would be more fun."

Rebecca was next. She went right up to the microphone. Then she whispered into it. She got all tongue-tied.

"Excuse me," said Echo Elmer with a smile. "This is radio—not a spy network. Tell us the name of your group."

Rebecca mumbled the name of her group. Suddenly Rebecca had turned very shy.

"You'll have to speak up."

"I don't think I can do this," admitted Rebecca. "I feel like I'm going to throw up."

"Try not to do it on the microphone," suggested Echo Elmer gently.

Rebecca came rushing out of the room. "How was it?" Sam asked.

Rebecca didn't answer. She ran for the bathroom.

"It must be harder than it seems," said Sam.

"Don't freeze the way you did when you were a snowflake," said Robert.

"Or stutter the way you did in the Children's Museum," said Mabel. "That was just a make-believe TV studio, and you trembled like a leaf."

"Thanks for the family support," muttered Sam.

"Sam Bamford! Sam Bamford!" shouted Echo Elmer.

Sam sat in front of the microphone. "I'm a little nervous," he confessed to Echo Elmer.

"That's natural," said Echo Elmer. "Perfectly natural. Sam Bamford . . . Sam Bamford . . . You're the boy who wrote me the letter. What's the song you want to introduce?"

"'Little Red Rooster' by Howlin' Wolf."

"Not many kids your age know Howlin' Wolf," said Echo Elmer.

"I didn't until you talked about him," admitted Sam. "But I looked up things about him and listened to his music. He's great. I also got Wolfman Jack's book out of the library. He was cool. Do you think he'd mind if I called myself Wolfman Sam?"

Echo Elmer smiled. "I think he would have been flattered—as long as you keep it just in the school. After all, there is really only one Wolfman! Okay, Sam, my man, you're on. Give it your best shot."

Sam rubbed his sweaty palms on his pants.

He took a deep breath. It didn't matter about his sweaty palms. This was radio. Nobody could see him sweat.

"This is Wolfman Sam coming to you from P.S. 11," said Sam, saying the words he had practiced all night. "I'm going to play you one of my favorite songs by the great blues singer Howlin' Wolf. In concert Howlin' Wolf would crawl and roll on the floor. Then he'd growl. Howlin' Wolf recorded for the same man who first recorded Elvis Presley. And everybody from the Rolling Stones to Led Zeppelin to the Grateful Dead played his songs. Here he is."

Sam put on the song. Echo Elmer was grinning from ear to ear.

"Wolfman Sam. You're my man! I want you to be the disc jockey for this school."

"You do? Have mercy!" shouted Sam.

Echo Elmer patted him on the back. "That's what the real Wolfman Jack said all the time."

"I know," said Sam.

5

The Wolfman Is a Jerk

Sam loved being on the radio. Every morning he started his radio show with his "signature" sound: a loud "Awoooooo!" Soon everybody at school was howling when they saw Sam.

"What's it like having a relative who's a wolf?" asked Armando as he passed Robert and Mabel on the way out of class. "Does that make you the little pups in the pack?"

"Very funny," said Robert. Robert was getting tired of everybody cheering for Sam as the Wolfman. Sam almost never had time for Robert anymore. At home Sam was either on the phone or locked up in his room, practicing his routine for the radio.

One night after dinner Robert knocked on Sam's door. Sam didn't answer, so Robert walked right in. B.B. King was singing in the background. Sam had the lights down low. He stared at the phone, trying to work up the nerve to call Rebecca and ask her to the Monster Mash.

"What're you doing?" asked Robert.

"Nothing," said Sam. He didn't want to tell his brother that he was going to call Rebecca. What if she said no? What if she really didn't like him? What if she laughed at him?

"I'm bored," said Robert. "I've got nothing to do either. Maybe we can do nothing together."

"Just because I'm not doing anything, it doesn't mean that I want to do it with you," said Sam. "That would be stupid."

"Don't call me stupid," argued Robert.

"I didn't call you stupid. I said you sounded stupid."

"Well, I think your music is stupid," said Robert.

"That's B.B. King and his guitar, Lucille. He's the greatest. Tomorrow I'm having an all–B.B. King day."

"Aren't you ever going to play anything good on the radio?" asked Robert.

"Wolfman Sam plays only the best," bragged Sam.

"You're letting all this wolf stuff go to your head."

"Did you know wolves are the most intelligent canines?" asked Sam. "I read about it in a book."

"Is that all you're doing? Reading a book about wolves? And you don't have time to play with me?"

"Play?" said Sam disdainfully. "The Wolfman doesn't have time to play. But I am thirsty. I'll have some apple juice."

"Go to the kitchen and get it," said Robert.

"You're the one with nothing to do. You can go get me a drink," said Sam.

Robert sighed. But he went to the kitchen.

Just after he poured the apple juice, the phone rang.

Robert picked up the phone. "Hello?" he said.

"Sam?" said a girl's voice. She sounded like she was out of breath.

"No, it's Robert."

"Oh, I wanted Sam. It's Rebecca."

Robert made a face. "Hey, Sam. It's for you!" he shouted. "Rebecca!"

Sam couldn't believe it. Rebecca had called *him*. What an act of fate! The Wolfman was on a roll. Nothing bad could happen to the Wolfman.

He grabbed the phone. "Hi, Rebecca," he said shyly. "I was just thinking about you." He nervously took a sip of the apple juice that Robert brought to him.

Robert couldn't believe his ears. His brother was admitting to a girl that he was thinking about her. Robert stared at his brother.

"Excuse me a minute, Rebecca," said Sam. "I have to get rid of a pest." He gave Robert a meaningful look. Robert didn't move.

"Well?" said Sam.

"Well what?"

"The Wolfman would like a little privacy."

"The Wolfman is a jerk," mumbled Robert.

Robert went to his room. He turned on his computer. He had forgotten that his encyclopedia CD-ROM was still in the player. Robert looked up Wolfman. There was nothing about disc jockeys, but a lot about werewolves. Robert read: *A werewolf is human being, man, woman or child, who willingly or unwillingly changes into the shape of a wolf.*

Man, woman, or child—well, Sam *was* a child, thought Robert.

Most werewolves turn back into normal people during the day, Robert read. Robert wondered about that—would anybody really call Sam normal? Probably not.

How to Identify a Werewolf

Robert studied the list.

1. *Werewolves like their meat rare.*
2. *They are always thirsty.*
3. *They sleep very soundly.*
4. *Their eyebrows tend to meet at a point over the nose.*

5. *Their ears are set far back on the head.*
6. *Werewolves hate the light.*
7. *Their power is greatest during a full moon, especially at harvesttime.*

Robert didn't know about Sam's ears, but he had noticed that Sam's eyebrows were looking a little wolflike lately.

Robert went back to Sam's room. Sam was still on the phone. He gave Robert a dirty look and waved him away. Sam shifted the phone from one ear to the other. Robert studied his brother's ear. It looked kind of flat and close to his head.

"Will you get out of here!" growled Sam.

Robert went back to his room and clicked in the instructions for the computer to print the article off the CD-ROM. He decided he'd better keep the list. A close-up picture of a werewolf printed out with the article. Robert studied it. Then he drew in a pair of glasses. It looked a lot like Sam.

Robert stuck his tongue out at the picture. Sam was being such a pain lately, it would serve

him right if he *did* turn into a werewolf. Then Robert giggled to himself. Maybe he could make Sam think he was a werewolf.

In the back of his desk drawer Robert found the leftover fake beard that he had used when he was playing Abe Lincoln.

"The Wolfman's brother gets revenge," mumbled Robert to himself.

He felt better than he had in a long time!

6

Me Wolfman— You Wolfwoman

That night Sam dreamed that there was a giant creature in bed with him. The creature had fleas and kept scratching itself. He woke up scratching himself.

Then he looked down at his bed. "Ma!" He rushed into the kitchen. Robert was all alone in the kitchen, eating a bowl of cereal.

"Where's Mom?" wailed Sam.

"She had to go to work early," said Robert. "What's wrong?"

"My bed!" said Sam. "Come look!"

Robert went to Sam's bed. There were hairs all over it.

"Wow!" said Robert. "You're shedding!"

"My thoughts exactly," said Sam. "First one hair under my arm, and now this. I'm shedding hair at night. What do you think it means?" Sam asked.

This was the opening Robert was hoping for. "Sam, have you ever considered that you could be a werewolf?"

"What?" exclaimed Sam.

"Maybe it's no accident that you became Wolfman Sam," said Robert.

Robert went to his room and came back with his list. "You've been eating your meat raw—and even eggs raw. You're thirsty. You like the dark. You hate to wake up in the morning. And now you're shedding."

Sam's heart was pounding. "What's that list?" he asked.

"I was just doing some research," said Robert.

"It's how to tell if you're a werewolf."

Sam studied the list. "This list is scary. I must have powerful hormones," said Sam quietly.

"What are hormones?" asked Robert.

Sam put his arm around his little brother. "Just hope that yours aren't like mine," he said. "I must have the biggest hormones in the world." Sam went to get dressed for school. Robert just shook his head and laughed.

Sam felt pumped up. At first the hairs in his bed had scared him. But now when he thought about it, it was a sign—a sign of his power. After all, wasn't everything going his way? He had wanted to be disc jockey, and of all the kids trying out, *he* had been chosen.

He had wanted to ask Rebecca to the Monster Mash, and *she* had asked him. The hair was a powerful omen.

At school Sam went straight to the room with the PA system. He grabbed the microphone. "Good morning! This is the Wolfman. I've got the spirit of the wolf in me today." Sam cupped his hands in front of his mouth, lifted his head back, and let out a loud "Awooooooo!"

After his show, Armando grinned at him.

"You were great," he said. Sam gave him a high five. Out in the hall Sam ran into Rebecca.

"Awooooo!" said Sam, throwing his head back and howling. "Me Wolfman. You Wolfwoman!"

Rebecca put her hands on her hips. She looked angry. "What did you say?"

"Uh . . . me Wolfman—you Wolfwoman?"

"That's the stupidest thing I've ever heard," said Rebecca. She went into class.

Sam was embarrassed. Suddenly he didn't feel quite so good about everything that was happening to him. He couldn't concentrate on the lesson. He didn't think anybody else was shedding hair at night. What if it was something more powerful than hormones? What if somehow he *did* have the power of a wolf inside him?

Ms. Perretti asked Sam a question. Sam blinked. He hadn't heard a word she had said. Sam heard titters behind him.

"Maybe the wolfboy can only howl," shouted one of his classmates.

Sam didn't trust himself to speak. What if they were right? What if he opened his mouth and started howling like a wolf? He was afraid to talk.

"Sam?" repeated Ms. Perretti.

Sam looked at Rebecca. She had gotten real mad at him when he had called her Wolfwoman. Sometimes he felt as if Rebecca could be his best friend in the world. And sometimes he felt that she hated him.

Ms. Perretti sighed. "Sam, I'd like to see you after class," she said.

Sam knew he had to get help somewhere.

"Ms. Perretti," asked Sam when they were alone, "what would happen to a kid who had really powerful hormones?"

Ms. Perretti narrowed her eyes. "What do you mean?"

"I think I have the hormones of a wolf," mumbled Sam.

"What?" asked Ms. Perretti.

"What if a kid—right about to jump into— uh, all those changes you were talking about— what if that kid became a wolf—instead of a man—or a wolfman?

"The way I see it," babbled Sam, "I took the personality of Wolfman Sam because Echo Elmer told us about Wolfman Jack and Howlin'

Wolf. Somehow I let the spirit of the wolf inside me, and now it's coming out, and I don't know how to get rid of it."

Ms. Perretti put up her hand. "Sam, it isn't like you to make silly jokes. I know kids have trouble with the whole subject of health and puberty—but it's important that you know how to take care of yourself. Now stop kidding around."

"I'm not kidding!" shouted Sam. "One day I'm a kid—and the next day I'm the Wolfman."

"Now Sam, try not to get carried away," said Ms. Perretti. "Though I do think it's wonderful that you're getting so involved in your radio program. And personally, I love the music that you play. It makes my day. You know, I can remember listening to the real Wolfman Jack myself when I was a kid. 'Have mercy!' That's what he always said."

Sam looked up at her. Who was going to have mercy on him?

Sam walked down the hall. He saw Rebecca staring at him with her friends. She started to giggle. Their giggles sounded horribly loud to Sam. He couldn't stand it.

He felt like a beast was lurking inside him—ready to pounce. Sam knew that he had to trust somebody with his secret. So he looked into his heart and thought about whom he could trust. The answer surprised him.

7

My Brother's
a Werewolf

Sam knocked on Robert's door.

"How's the Wolfman doing?" asked Robert.

Robert's gerbils, Exterminator and Terminator, jumped onto the wheel in their cage and started spinning around faster and faster. "Even my gerbils try to run away from you," teased Robert.

"Animals are smart," said Sam. "They can

sense when something is wrong." To Robert's dismay Sam had tears in his eyes.

"Sam, what's wrong?" asked Robert.

"Can you keep a secret?" Sam asked.

Robert nodded.

"I might really be a werewolf," Sam whispered.

Robert tried to keep a straight face. Sam could see that he wanted to laugh.

"I'm serious, man," said Sam. "I've got weird urges and appetites."

"Just because of a few hairs in your bed . . . "

Sam sat down at Robert's desk. Then he saw the picture of the werewolf with glasses that Robert had made.

"That's me!" screamed Sam.

"Uh, Sam," said Robert, "take it easy."

Sam licked his lips. "Could you get me a drink of water?" he asked Robert.

Robert stared at his brother. "You're thirsty again?"

Sam nodded. "And I'm hungry."

"Sam, you don't really think you're a werewolf, do you? I mean that drawing was just something I did to fool around. It's not . . . "

"It's not what?" asked Sam.

"It's just a drawing I did," confessed Robert.

"Yes, but why?" asked Sam. "You're my brother. We have the same blood. Something inside you made you do this drawing of me."

"Uh, Sam, I think you're going off the deep end with this."

"Am I?" said Sam. "It's the beast within me." Sam paced around the room. Robert watched. It was more like a lope than a pace. "I told you before that wolves are one of the smartest animals in the wild," Sam said. He looked down at his belly as if expecting to see the wolf lurking there. He felt that the wolf inside him was a particularly smart one.

"I'm scared, Robert," Sam confessed. "There are things inside me that I can't control. . . . You have to face it. Your brother's a werewolf. I'll have to be careful not to let the wolf out. I could hurt somebody."

Mrs. Bamford called them to help set the table. Mabel and her family were coming for dinner. When Mabel and her family arrived, Mrs. Bamford greeted them with a kiss. Mabel was dressed all in red. Mabel waited for Sam to tell her that she looked like a tomato, because he was always comparing her to a vegetable. But Sam shocked her. "You look nice, Mabel," Sam said.

"What's going on with Sam?" Mabel whispered to Robert. "He was nice to me."

Robert scratched his head. He didn't know how to tell Mabel that his brother was being extra nice so the werewolf inside him wouldn't come out.

"I hope you're hungry," shouted Mrs. Bamford as she went to the kitchen. "We don't have red meat much anymore, but Sam's been asking for steak. And this morning I had a craving, too." She brought out a platter with a gigantic sirloin steak, so big that its edges hung over the plate.

"Oh, yuck!" said Mabel. "I don't eat meat."

"Mabel, dear, we don't say 'yuck' at the table," said Mabel's mother, but she was looking at the steak as if it might jump off the table and bite her. "I don't eat red meat either, but I'm sure there's plenty else to eat."

"Wow, Mom! Steak!" shouted Sam. He ate

with particular gusto. All the Bamfords had juicy red steak; Mabel and her mother and father ate nothing but the vegetables and greens, plus big helpings of chocolate cake.

After dinner Mabel asked to play with Robert's gerbils. She got them out of the cage. "Hi, cuties!" she exclaimed. Sam and Robert made a face. They didn't like Termie and Extermie being called cute.

Mabel cuddled them, stroking their furry little heads. "You poor little babies. Do you know what Sam and Robert did? They ate moo-moo."

"Will you stop talking baby talk to the gerbils?" said Sam. His voice cracked. It came out as a little bit of a growl.

Mabel looked hurt. "Stop growling at me!" she insisted.

"Did I growl?" asked Sam in a scared voice.

"It did sound a little like a growl," said Robert. Mabel cuddled the gerbils closer.

"Mabel, maybe you should take the gerbils home to stay with you for a couple of days," said Sam.

"What are you talking about?" asked Robert.

Sam was looking at the gerbils thoughtfully. "Hungry wolves sometimes go after small game."

"Have you gone loco?" Robert asked his brother.

"Loco or lobo?" asked Sam nervously.

"Lobo is Spanish for wolf," whispered Mabel.

"Exactly," said Sam. "Mabel, get the gerbils out of here. They aren't safe around me. Robert, you have to face it. Our whole family may be infected. You drew that picture of me. Mom made a steak and we all ate it. We might come from a whole line of secret werewolves."

Mabel was staring at her older cousin with round eyes.

"Mabel," said Sam, "because you are family, I will tell you. But you must never tell anybody. A wolf is inside me. I don't know if I can control it."

"Sam, you're a disc jockey—not a wolf," protested Robert.

"We don't know that for sure," said Sam, looking at the gerbils a little hungrily. "I think we should show Mabel that list."

Robert got out his "How to Identify a Werewolf" list. Mabel looked at it over Sam's shoulder.

"I'll put a check mark next to all the ones that fit," said Sam.

✔1. *Werewolves like their meat rare.*
✔2. *They are always thirsty.*
✔3. *They sleep very soundly.*
✔4. *Their eyebrows tend to meet at a point over the nose.*
✔5. *Their ears are set far back on the head.*
✔6. *Werewolves hate the light.*
  7. *Their power is greatest during a full moon, especially at harvesttime.*

"See," said Sam. "Six out of seven must mean something. And it's the fall—harvesttime."

"In school we're studying Halloween," said Mabel. "We learned that Halloween is partly a harvest festival."

"That's all I need," groaned Sam.

"You could be looking at this the wrong way," said Mabel. "Wolves can be very friendly. I've read lots of good things about wolves."

"Get a life, Mabel," growled Sam. "The wolf inside me isn't friendly."

Mabel held the gerbils even closer to her. She agreed to take them home—for their safety and for her own.

8

Save the Wolf

A couple of days before Halloween Mrs. Bamford pulled a slip out of her purse. "Sam, remember to go to the costume store to pick up your costume. It's your responsibility."

Sam stared at her blankly.

"How could you forget? It's the wolf costume that you wanted for Halloween," said Mrs. Bamford. "What's wrong with you boys? Usually you're so excited about Halloween.

Sam, you've been talking about the Monster Mash for a month. And Robert, Willie is going to take you and Mabel trick-or-treating."

"On Halloween I might not need a costume," said Sam. His mother looked at him curiously.

When they got to school, Armando came up to Sam. "Don't forget—we said we'd all go to the Monster Mash together. It'll be great. There's going to be a full moon."

Sam's eyes got big. "A full moon?" he gasped. "Rebecca might not be safe."

Armando laughed. "Because you're the Wolfman?"

"It's not funny," hissed Sam. "The combination of the harvest and a full moon could be fatal for friends of the Wolfman."

"The harvest? You're in the middle of New York City. Just avoid the farmers' markets. What's with you?" demanded Armando. "Are you getting cold feet about going with Rebecca? A wolf like you shouldn't worry."

"Stop calling me a wolf," snapped Sam.

"I meant it as a compliment," said Armando.

"It's not—at least not the way you meant it," said Sam.

Sam went into the room with the PA system. Usually that was the one place that he felt at home. Sam sat at the microphone. He stared at it. "Good morning, folks. It's Sam." Sam's voice was barely above a whisper. He sounded like a little kid. "I'm going to play you a Muppet medley today. First we have Kermit's song." Then he pushed the button to play the songs he had brought from home.

Rebecca was waiting for him when he came out of the booth. "A Muppet medley! Since when does the Wolfman play Muppet songs?"

"I like Muppet songs," said Sam in a low voice.

Rebecca rolled her eyes. "Where did the Wolfman go?" she asked.

"I didn't feel like being the Wolfman today."

"Well, I hope the Wolfman comes back for the Monster Mash. You're so cute when you get all wolflike. I hope you have a werewolf costume like you promised."

"Rebecca, it's a full moon the night of the Monster Mash. It might be dangerous. And it's harvesttime."

Rebecca stared at him blankly.

"You didn't like it when I said 'Me Wolfman—You Wolfwoman,'" Sam reminded her.

"You sounded like a jerk when you said that. But I still like the Wolfman." Rebecca smiled at him and walked away.

Sam walked down the hall, feeling confused. He stopped at the water fountain.

"Hey, Wolfman, what was that music you played this morning? It stank," shouted one of the fifth graders.

Sam took a long drink of water. Mabel came up to him. "I liked the songs you played today," she said. "They were the kind of songs that a nice wolf would play."

"Oh, Mabel," groaned Sam. "Stop trying to make me feel better. There is no such thing as a nice wolf. I'd do anything not to be a werewolf. But nobody can help me. I'm a danger to myself and others."

Mabel ran to Robert. "Sam seems to be getting worse. We have to help Sam right away. We're his pack."

"His what?" asked Robert.

"We're his pack," repeated Mabel. "Wolves

live in packs with close family ties. They take care of their young and old—and nearly everything wolves do, they do together. Wolves depend on their families. You and I are Sam's closest relatives—so it's our duty as part of his pack to help him. I've been doing my own research. On how to cure a werewolf."

"How do you do that?" asked Robert.

"I got a book from the library. *Meet the Werewolf* by Georgess McHargue. In order to cure a werewolf, you draw a circle on the ground about seven feet across and put the werewolf in the middle of it. Then you have to hit him with a twig from an ash tree. Do you know where to find an ash tree?"

Robert scratched his head. "Well, we have a fireplace. What if we put ashes on some twigs from the park?"

"That might work," said Mabel. "There's a lot of other stuff we'll need. I'm making a list. We need vinegar to make some bad-smelling goo to pour on him. What else smells bad?"

"The nuts from the ginkgo trees stink," said Robert. "There are lots of ginkgo trees in the park."

"Great," said Mabel. "You know, Robert, you're very good at this. We can do the whole thing in Central Park. I think it will be better if we do it outside. The spirits will be with us. It could even be fun. But do you think Sam wants to be cured?"

"I don't know," said Robert thoughtfully.

9

A Matter of Wolf or Death

Sam felt weird when he picked up the wolf costume that he was renting. "You're lucky you ordered early," said the man at the costume store. "We've had a last-minute rush on wolves this year—probably because it's a full moon for Halloween."

"Don't remind me," said Sam. "I'm hoping for rain."

"Rain?" scoffed the man. "It's supposed to be a beautiful night. There won't be any rain on Halloween."

"Just my luck," said Sam. The clerk put the costume in a plastic bag and handed it to Sam.

When he got home, he put on his werewolf costume. He went to the bathroom to look at himself in the mirror. He had to admit that he kind of liked the way he looked. His shoulders were broad from the pads—and even the wolflike head was sort of noble.

Sam was still admiring himself in the mirror when Mabel and Robert walked in on him.

"I think we're too late," said Mabel.

"What do you want?" Sam asked.

"We're here to help," said Robert. "Mabel thinks she's found a way to help you not be a werewolf anymore. We'll drive the wolf out of you with a special ceremony. But you have to come to the park with us."

Sam took one last look at himself in the mirror as a werewolf.

Robert stared at his brother. Robert felt that he could read Sam's mind. That happens between brothers sometimes. "Do you want to stay this way?" Robert asked Sam softly.

"If I could be sure that it was just a costume," sighed Sam. "But it's more than that. It's the werewolf inside me that I'm worried about. We'd better do the ceremony."

"All right!" said Mabel. "Robert, you get ashes from the fireplace. I'll get the vinegar. As soon as we get to the park, we'll start grinding up gingko nuts."

"What's she talking about?" asked Sam.

"The cure!" said Robert. "Big Bro—you're going to be cured."

Sam looked at his brother suspiciously. It seemed to Sam that Robert and Mabel might be enjoying themselves a little too much.

Mabel carried the book into the park. People barely glanced at Sam in his werewolf costume. One kid on skates waved, but most people didn't seem to notice.

"You'd think people saw werewolves every day," complained Mabel.

"This is New York, kid," said Robert. "The Big Enchilada. These people have seen everything."

Mabel glanced down at the book. "It says

here to take the werewolf to a lonely spot and tie it up."

"I'm not letting you tie me up," said Sam emphatically. "And I'm definitely not going to a lonely spot."

"Maybe we should do it in Sheep Meadow," suggested Robert.

"Great idea," said Mabel. "After all, wolves love sheep. My mom read me a story about a wolf in sheep's clothing."

"And here we have a sheep dressed up as a wolf," said Robert, pointing to his brother.

"Hey!" said Sam. He didn't like being called a sheep.

"Okay," said Mabel in her bossy way when they arrived at Sheep Meadow. "Let's get this show on the road." She got a stick and drew a circle in the dirt. "Stand in the middle of the circle," she ordered Sam.

"Who put her in charge?" asked Sam.

"Well, she is part of your pack," said Robert.

"Okay—now the oldest one trying to cure the werewolf has to kick him," said Mabel.

"What!" exclaimed Sam

"I'm older than Mabel. I get to do it," said

Robert gleefully. "Just remember, Sam, I'm doing this for your own good."

Robert took a few steps back to get a running start.

"Wait a minute. Wait a minute!" said Sam. "If I'm a werewolf, Robert could be a werewolf too. We're brothers."

Mabel looked down at her book. "He's right, you know. Maybe for good luck I should kick both of you. I'm just a cousin, so I'm probably safe."

Before Robert and Sam could object, Mabel gave them each a quick kick in the butt.

Sam growled. "Maybe I should stay a werewolf and eat her."

"I'm kind of going to miss my brother as a werewolf," said Robert.

Mabel put her hands on her hips. "Will you two take this seriously or not?"

"Not!" said Sam and Robert together. They giggled.

Mabel glared at Sam. "Sam Bamford, do you really want to remain a werewolf? A threat to yourself and to others—a freak of nature?"

Sam swallowed hard. He thought about it.

He and Robert might kid around, but it wasn't fun being scared about being a werewolf. He thought about the upcoming dance with Rebecca. It wouldn't be any fun to have to go to the dance as a freak.

"I don't want to be a werewolf," said Sam. "Go on with the spell."

"Good," said Mabel. "No more fooling around."

Sam did as he was told. Mabel got the mashed ginkgo nuts that Robert had gathered. She mixed them with the vinegar. She started to pour the goo on Sam. "No way," said Sam. "You're not pouring that on my costume. I'll stink at the Monster Mash."

Mabel gave him a dirty look. "It says here that everybody who wants to cure the werewolf is supposed to dip cups into bad-smelling goo and pour it on the werewolf."

Sam stuck out one paw. "You can pour it on one paw! One paw!"

"That should be okay," said Robert. "After all, he's just a kid—it probably doesn't take the whole spell."

Mabel looked a little doubtful. She took two

twigs and dipped them into the ashes Robert had brought. She gave one twig to Robert and then stepped into the circle, shaking her twig at Sam and chanting.

"Graywolf ugly, graywolf old,
Do at once as you are told.
Leave this man and fly away—
Right away, far away,
Where it's night and never day."

A woman carrying a briefcase, riding a bicycle through the park, stopped to watch. "That's the spell to cure a werewolf, isn't it?" she asked.

Mabel nodded. "How did you know?" she asked.

"I'm a witch," said the woman in a calm voice. She smiled and got back on her bike.

"New York is weird," said Mabel.

10

The Wolfman
Has a Good Time

On the day of the Monster Mash, Armando and Rebecca came to pick Sam up. Rebecca was dressed like a pirate. Unfortunately, so was Mabel.

"I'm a pirate queen," said Rebecca proudly.

"What does that make me, a pirate princess?" asked Mabel. "No way. You-ho! You-ho!"

"I think it's supposed to be 'Yo-ho-ho!'" said Robert.

Sam came out dressed in his chinos and a T-shirt. Rebecca looked at him disappointedly. "Where's your costume?" she asked.

Sam shrugged.

"Aren't you going to put it on?" asked Rebecca. "You're going as the Wolfman, aren't you?"

"Rebecca, I . . . Tonight I thought maybe I should just go as Sam Bamford. That's my costume."

"But I asked you because you're the Wolfman!" said Rebecca.

"Sam Bamford's really not so bad," said Robert.

"Of course he's not. But he can't go to a costume party like that," said Rebecca. "Now put on your costume, Sam, and let's go."

Sam went into his room. Robert followed him. Sam put on the hairy leggings that came with the costume. "Cool," said Robert. "So now that you're cured, you're going to have a great time, right?"

Sam shook his head. "What if the cure didn't

work?" he asked. "Maybe I should have let Mabel pour all that ginkgo juice over me."

"If you had, you would have stunk up the whole school," said Robert. "The smell is bad enough just on that one paw."

"I think I should have let Mabel do the whole thing," said Sam. "After all, I have powerful werewolf hormones. Remember the wolf hairs that we found in my bed."

Before Robert could say anything, Armando knocked on the door. "Ready, buddy? We don't want to be late. What's that smell?" asked Armando.

"Ginkgo juice," said Sam. He gave Robert his paw. "Wish me luck, brother," he said. "I hope I don't ruin everything."

Robert bit his lip. He wished that he'd had time to tell his brother the truth.

After the older kids left, Mabel told Robert to stop standing around like a dolt. "It's time for us to go trick-or-treating!" said Mabel. "Put on your costume."

Robert put on a gorilla mask. "You look adorable," said Mrs. Bamford. There was a knock on the door. It was Willie, the Bamfords' neighbor. He was dressed up as a zombie. Even though he was already in junior high, he had come to take Mabel and Robert out trick-or-treating.

"Hey, what's the matter, man?" Willie asked Robert. "You look like a sad-sack gorilla."

"I'm worried about Sam," said Robert. "Even though Mabel did a cure, he still thinks he's a werewolf."

"As the person in charge of the cure, I should do a follow-up checkup on Sam. Otherwise, I might be sued for bad werewolf curing," declared Mabel.

"What are you two talking about?" asked Willie.

"We want to go to the Monster Mash," said Robert. "But we're not supposed to because we're not in the fourth or fifth grade."

"The Monster Mash," said Willie with a sigh. "I remember it well."

"Then you'll have no trouble helping us sneak in," said Mabel.

"Well," said Willie, "everybody will be in

costume. And I think I can get us in. But we shouldn't stay too long."

"It's a matter of wolf or death," said Mabel.

Willie took Mabel and Robert, dressed in their costumes, to school. In the gymnasium they could hear a very familiar voice saying, *"It's Echo Elmer, Echo Elmer! Coming to you live—from the scene of his youth—the Monster Mash at P.S. 11. Where the monsters come out to play—play—play— PLAY!"* Echo Elmer's voice bounced off the walls of the gymnasium. He put on Ray Charles singing "Let the Good Times Roll."

Mabel and Robert made their way through the crowd. Robert spotted Sam standing by himself against the wall. He didn't look like he was having a very good time. Robert turned to Mabel. "I think I'd better try to talk to Sam by myself," he said. He walked over to Sam.

Sam looked up and saw him.

"Say, buddy, want to do the werewolf shuffle?" the gorilla asked.

Sam shook his head no.

"You're not exactly the life of the party," said the gorilla.

"I know," growled Sam. "But this is the only way I can keep everybody safe. I invited the spirit of the wolf into my soul, and it took over. I tried to be cured, but I'm afraid it didn't work."

Robert lifted his mask. "Sam, it's me. Robert. You shouldn't talk that way, especially to strangers. You weren't ever really a werewolf. I put those hairs in your bed. They came from my Abe Lincoln beard. You were making such a big deal about your underarm hair and everything, I just wanted to teach you a lesson."

"You mean I didn't have to go through all that stuff in the park—the ginkgo juice and those twigs in my face, and Mabel kicking me in the rear?"

"She kicked me, too," said Robert. "And I never even claimed to be a werewolf."

"Where is she?" Sam demanded.

"She's over against the wall—with the zombie," said Robert. "She doesn't know I started this. She's just worried that the cure didn't work—that you still think you're a were-wolf."

"I could be," said Sam.

"But I told you that it was me who put the hair in your bed," said Robert.

"That's just one thing. But what about all the other things on your list? The wolf inside me could still be waiting to come out."

Robert looked at his brother to see if he was kidding or not. Robert couldn't tell.

Suddenly Sam and Robert heard a loud voice coming over the loudspeakers. "Say, Wolfman Sam! How about coming over and giving a Wolfman howl to all your fans?"

Rebecca came over to get Sam. "It's being broadcast live all over the city," she said. "You gotta be the Wolfman!"

Sam looked at his brother. Then he went to the microphone. "Awoooooo!" he howled into the mike. Echo Elmer patted him on the back. "The Wolfman lives! The Wolfman lives!"

Mabel made her way up to the front. She looked worried.

"Was that Sam howling?" she asked the gorilla.

Robert nodded.

Sam stepped down from the stage. "Sam?" asked Mabel nervously. "Are you okay?"

"The Wolfman lives!" said Sam. And then he winked at Robert.

"Oh no," said Mabel. "Our cure didn't work."

"I'm not sure," said Robert. He wondered about that wink. Did werewolves wink? And if they did, what did it mean?

Sam was dancing and howling away. He looked like a werewolf having a very good time.